DAYLAN
AND THE
RIVER OF
SECRETS

EDD TELLO

An imprint of Enslow Publishing

WEST **44** BOOKS™

Please visit our website, www.west44books.com.
For a free color catalog of all our high-quality books,
call toll free 1-800-398-2504.

Cataloging-in-Publication Data
Names: Tello, Edd.
Title: Daylan and the river of secrets / Edd Tello.
Description: Buffalo, NY : West 44, 2025. | Series: West 44 MG verse
Identifiers: ISBN 9781978597488 (pbk.) | ISBN 9781978597471 (library
bound) | ISBN 9781978597495 (ebook)
Subjects: LCSH: Swimming--Juvenile fiction. | Divorce--Juvenile fiction. |
Families--Juvenile fiction. | Mexico--Juvenile fiction. | Friendship--Juvenile
fiction.
Classification: LCC PZ7.1.T455 Da 2025 | DDC [F]--dc23

First Edition

Published in 2025 by
Enslow Publishing
2544 Clinton Street
Buffalo, NY 14224

Editor: Caitie McAneney
Designer: Tanya Dellaccio Keeney

Photo Credits: Cover (texture) Bodor Tivadar/Shutterstock.com.

Printed in the United States of America

CPSIA compliance information: Batch #CS25W44: For further information contact
Enslow Publishing LLC at 1-800-398-2504.

Find us on

This book is a gift to El Mante, the town where I was born and have lived most of my life. I wrote this story as a thanks to those who have shown me how essential and mythical El Nacimiento (the birthplace) is to our community and its history.
May its cave continue to be explored.
May the song of its waters be heard forever.

GLOSSARY

abuela: Grandmother.

abuelo: Grandfather.

ándale: "Come on."

a ver: "Let's see"

caldo de res: A Mexican beef and vegetable soup.

chanclas: Slippers or flip-flops.

copal: Scented smoke.

huizache: A common shrub or small tree with light green foliage.

La Chalupa: A character card from the Mexican lotería card deck featuring a lady in a canoe-like boat.

lancha: Fishing boat mostly used by Mexican fishermen.

leyendas mexicanas: Mexican legends.

mijo: My son.

¿neta?: "Really? Are you serious?"

palapa: A traditional Mexican shelter roofed with palm leaves or branches.

todo está bien: "Everything's okay."

SOMEDAY

I dip my toes into
the green-blue water.
Then my whole body

sinks.

I'm no longer
Scaredy Daylan.
I flutter kick.
My arms move in circles
in the cold river.

I float.

The warm rays of the sun
shine on my face.

I dive.

"Daylan Torres, it's five.
Time to go!"

I open my eyes.

I am still sitting on the stones.

Mamá hugs me from behind.
Her long straight hair falls on my
sweaty forehead.

Someday, I tell myself.
Someday, I will dive into the river again.

NEWBORNS

I put my life jacket and
goggles in the trunk.
Mom towel-dries her hair.

By the way she stares at me,
I know she's worried.
I know both she and Papá
would like me to swim again.
It's been three years.

In San José Lagos,
water is sacred.
We swim from the time we are born.
Parents put their babies
in the clean waters of
the Nacimiento River.

>Nacimiento means "birth."
>People here also
>call the river El Naci.

I get into the car—
the same gray car
that Papá used to drive
before he left home.

CULEBRA

Dad left home
when I was nine.

For several months,
my parents' screams
were like a culebra
—a water snake.
They wound around my neck.

The fights happened more and more.
I felt as if a culebra
was dragging me
to the depths of El Naci.

One sunny afternoon,
Dad took me out
in this same car.

He said, sobbing,
"Sometimes relationships
don't work out.
You'll understand
when you grow up."

It's been three years,
and I still don't get it.

That day, when I got home,
I ran to my room
and cried.

I cried so much
that I could have filled
El Nacimiento.

Mamá came
and talked to me
about things
I didn't understand.

Marriage agreements,
divorce papers,
a guardian.

All I knew was
that I didn't want
Papá to leave.

Mom and I stayed in
San José Lagos.
Papá moved to
Mexico City,
eight hours
from here.

WHY I
STOPPED SWIMMING

Mamá calls them
"Rainy Days"—
those days
when I feel
anxious or sad.

One of those days
right after Papá left,
Mamá took me to
El Naci.

Heat was sticky.
The water
was cold.

Mom stayed
on shore
with Trueno,
our dog.

As I floated,
I felt something
spinning
under me.

At first,
I didn't freak out.
Coach Irma,
our PE teacher,
had told us:
When water flows
in a narrow space,
it can collide
with a slower
stream of water.
It forms a whirlpool.

But when I dove
under the surface,
I saw a woman's
white face.
Almost see-through.
She looked
like she was dead.

I saw her eyes,
but not her body.

I saw her arms,
but not her legs.

I rose to the surface.
I shouted.

Trueno barked
and ran
to the shore.

And I'm very
VERY sure
of what I saw:
the tip of a fish tail
sticking out
of the water.

Trueno saw it, too.
Mamá didn't.

She was staring at me.
She was scared
by my screams.

The whirlpool
disappeared,
but my body
kept shaking.

Since that afternoon,

> I haven't gone
> swimming
> like I used to.

After that,

> I started
> having nightmares.
> I dreamed
> a fish lady
> dragged me down
> into the depths of
> El Nacimiento.

But when I stopped
swimming,
the bad dreams
were gone.

So I'll never swim
again.

TRUENO

rushes at me
as I get out of the car.

I don't know
what breed he is.
Dad and I adopted him
when he was a puppy.

Dad and I named him *Trueno*,
which means "thunder,"
because he runs very fast.

Trueno is dark brown
like my hair color.
He listens with pointy ears.
Trueno is thin like me.

Trueno was the only one
who saw the Patroness of Water,
Cihuamichin.

He's the only other one
who knows her secret.

I hug Trueno
before going inside.

THE PROTECTOR OF OUR WATERS

In San José Lagos,
we honor Cihuamichin.
She's the protector
of our waters.

According to tradition,
          Cihuamichin
          gives humans
          great harvests.
          She is sometimes
          shown as a fish lady.

Some people even ask
for a miracle.

Every year,
believers and nonbelievers
prepare for the
Celebrations of Cihuamichin.
They make offerings of
food, flowers, and candles.

So it was expected
that one day
she would show up.

A PHASE

When I told Mamá
I had seen Cihuamichin,
she sighed. She said,
"Ay, Day.
It's just a legend
of a fish lady
among the townspeople, okay?"

When I told Papá
over the phone, he giggled.
He said, "Oh! You did?!"

The sound of his voice
told me he didn't
believe me either.
He didn't care.
He only cared
about me
swimming again.

When I told
Teacher Lily,
she said,
"It is surely just a story
you have heard."

Later, she asked Mamá
to stay at the end
of class.

She explained that imagining
nonexistent things
was a way of dealing
with the divorce.
Especially at my age.

That it would
give me comfort,
and it would
only be "a phase."

Ugh. Adults.

Then I went to
Brissia Olvera,
my only and
best friend.

She did not tell me
Cihuamichin
didn't exist.
But I could tell
she didn't believe me.

For a while,
I thought it was
my imagination.

But then I moved
on to sixth grade.

I met Teacher Alfonso,
and everything I knew
about
Cihuamichin
changed forever.

It wasn't just a phase
after all.

MONDAY AT SCHOOL

means wearing
navy blue trousers,
a uniform shirt,
and well-cleaned shoes.

"I put your sandwich
in your lunch box!"
Mom yells as
I walk to the school doors.

"I—I know," I stammer.

At least she's not
blowing kisses
at me anymore.

Mom is a counselor
at a high school.
She believes that's why
she always
says the "right words."

Brissia's eyes
are glued to a page
as I enter
our classroom.

Brissia is the town's
star swimmer.

Before even
saying hello,
she says,
with a smile that
shows her braces,
"Look, look!"

She hands me
the page:

**THE SCHOOL INVITES YOU TO
THE OPEN WATER
SWIMMING COMPETITION**

Another thing
to stress about
besides math.

Brissia thinks
she can help me
swim again.
I'm not sure
about that.

MONDAY MORNINGS

mean doing the flag ceremony outside.
But they also mean
Spanish literature,
my favorite class,
at 9:00 a.m.

Teacher Alfonso's eyes gleam
with excitement when
he tells us stories—
myths and legends.
They remind me of
my *abuelo's* eyes.

Teacher Alfonso
takes his glasses off.
We listen.

My favorite project
this year was:

> "Myths and Legends
> of the
> Mexican Oral Tradition."

In teams, we researched about
leyendas mexicanas.

CIHUAMICHIN

Brissia and I
shared with the class
the legend of
Cihuamichin.

I said,
"Of all the stories
Abuelo told me,
this was my favorite.
It goes something like this:

A long time ago,
where San José de Lagos
is now located,
there was a region
surrounded by
rivers and lagoons.

The waters had been
entrusted to
Cihuamichin,
a deity.
Half woman, half fish.

She ruled
this region.

She spent her days
collecting
garbage that
people
threw into
the river,
and protecting
fish, crayfish,
and other creatures.

She only surfaced
to collect
fruit and herbs.

Townspeople
made her
a bronze crown
with quartz,
fire opal, and
amber stones.
She gratefully
wore it.

They looked in awe.
Especially when
they heard her
singing."

"But breaking her rules
was dangerous," Brissia said.

"People knew abusing
her waters or harming
the beings that lived there
had a consequence.
For those offenders,
Cihuamichin
would entangle them
and drag them to the depths.
Forever."

Our classmates' eyes
were open wide.

"People claim that they still
hear her singing."

I added,
"Since then, we honor
Cihuamichin
as our Patroness of Water
every summer.
We ask her for a year of
abundance for us
and for our rivers."

After our research,
I had a lot
of questions.
But I only asked Teacher Alfonso
one of them.

"If I told you
I saw her
three years ago
in the river,
would you
believe me?"

He smiled.

"Daylan, if you had
told your abuelo
that you had seen her,
he would
have believed you.

Legends run
from generation
to generation
for a reason,
so yes. I believe you."

I started
dreaming about
her again.

This time,
I was floating,
lying in
the water.

At night,
it looked like a
different world
than the one
in daylight.

The turquoise
water turned
black.

I heard the chirping
of crickets
and the
croaking of frogs.

I recognized
Cihuamichin's
fish tail as it
moved swiftly.

"Come here,"
she said.

First,
I got scared.

> Her voice
> was not as soft
> as I had
> imagined it
> to be. It was raspy.

Then,
I obeyed.

> I held onto her tail.
> It was not slimy.

> Rather,
> it seemed
> made of
> ceramic and
> resin.

In my nightmares,
she was a
fast swimmer.

"STOP!"
I would yell.

She didn't stop
and seemed
to enjoy it.

It wasn't
drowning that
terrified me.

It was me
breaking her rules.

Then her
fish tail would
turn into a reptile's tail
and she would
bite me.

BACK TO THE PRESENT

After flag ceremony,
we open our
reading books.

Before starting,
Principal Concepción
enters the classroom
with a boy next to her.

She says,
"Good morning, class.
This is Eliam Salazar."

Teacher Alfonso
tells us the new guy
comes from another school.
He will finish
the school year with us.

Eliam's walnut eyes look sleepy.
His messy hair
dances across his forehead.

I can tell that he just
wants to sit down.

Some of the girls
whisper to each other
and giggle.

He slumps in a seat.

I notice a scar
running from
his eyebrow
to his hair.

I have
many questions.

*How did he get
that scar?
Why did he enroll in
this school?
Why just now when
there are less
than two months to go
before the
school year ends?*

LITTLE STRAWS

Sports aren't my thing.
Nothing
played in
a team.

The only sport
I really
liked was
swimming.

I could slip
into the water
and move freely.

But when Coach Irma
blows
her whistle,
my hands fiddle
with my
notebook.

I stand up
and my legs
shake.

My legs
are so thin that
my classmates
call them
popotitos,
"little straws."

But in the water,
they used to
be so fast
that they could
look like
a fish tail.

27

"Guys,
I'll be waiting
for you
on the field!"
Coach Irma
tells us.

I'm nervous,
thinking that
the new kid
Eliam
will find out

I'm not good
at sports.

NOBODY PICKS ME

After putting on
our PE uniforms,
we are

        divided into
        two groups:
        one for girls,
        one for boys.

Coach Irma then
hands over
two soccer balls.

        One to Enrique
        and the other
        to Brissia.

Great.
My worst sport.

We divide
ourselves
into two teams.

Enrique is taller
than me.
He's the captain
of one team.

Germán has
green, catlike eyes.
He's the captain
of another team.

The rest of us
line up.

Neither of the captains
says my name.

I sweat
from
the June heat.

I sweat
because no one
chooses me.

If I was
in the girl group,
Brissia would
pick me
for her team.

NOT GOOD AT SPORTS

The goalie kicks the ball.
It falls near me.
I am a statue.
Players come and go.

"If you're not
going to play, just leave,"
Enrique yells at me.

Eliam watches me,
then he moves the ball
past Enrique, toward Tavo.
Tavo kicks the ball
hard and scores a goal.

Germán and his team
jump and scream.
Enrique gives me that
it's your fault look.

I get it.
I am not good at sports.

I'm not good
like my father was
when he was my age.

BAD NEWS

We return to the classroom.

Coach Irma informs us:

"Kids, listen.
Cihuamichin Night Celebration
is in two weeks,
so I have two pieces
of news for you.
One is good and one is not so good.
Which one
do you want
to hear first?"

"The bad one," Enrique replies.

"The 'not so good'
is that we will do
a general cleaning
in and around
El Nacimiento
this weekend."

My classmates
groan.

Coach Irma sighs.
"Hey, calm down.
There's a good one.
This activity will count
towards the final grade and—"

"Is that the good one?"
Enrique interrupts.

She says,
"Well, the good news
is that after you clean up,
you will have permission
to swim."

A shout
goes up.

Even Eliam,
who just arrived today,
beams with excitement.

I breathe out.
That would be
no problem if
I could just
swim again.

Teacher Alfonso
explains a math
problem that
no one
seems to
understand.

I draw fish
all over the page.

I would like
to draw
Cihuamichin, too.

But she is my secret.

I feel
a mass of hair
on my cheek
and neck.

I shudder.

It's Brissia's
curly hair.
She wants to laugh,
but only whispers,

"Don't worry,
Day. I'll help you
get back
to swimming
again.
How about
we practice
this afternoon?"

She knows me well.

"I have to think
about that,"
I say.

Brissia gives
me a big smile.

But no matter
how hard she tries
with me,

I know
I'm just not good
at sports—
on the field
or in the water.

BAD IDEA

At lunch,
Brissia and I
sit on the bench
under an old pine tree.

As I take my sandwich out,
I remember Teacher Alfonso
asked us to be nice to Eliam.

I imagine being the New Guy
must be hard.

Even when I'm not
the new one, it's hard.

Sometimes I don't even
want to come to school
when I think of
Enrique and Germán.

They tease me
by saying that
I only hang out
with girls.

What's the problem with that?

"Do you mind
if we invite
Eliam to lunch
with us?"
I ask Brissia.

She unwraps
her flour tacos.
"What for?"

I shrug. "I think maybe . . ."

Before
I can finish
the sentence, Brissia
points to Eliam.

He's playing
football on the field
with Germán, Enrique,
and the others.

Oh.

"Nevermind,"
I say.

MY BEST FRIEND

I'm finishing homework
in the dining room.
Outside, someone yells,
"Daaaay!" It's Brissia.

Trueno wags his tail and barks.

I hear Mamá's
chanclas coming
down the stairs
to open the door.

Brissia drops to her knees
and hugs Trueno.

"I thought you'd forget,"
I tell her.
"You have swim practice today."

She shrugs.
"I can take one day to help
my best friend get back to—"

"Brissia, I—"

Before I finish,
Mom sets
two glasses
of lemonade on
the wooden table,
grinning.

One thing
about Brissia:

                she never forgets
                the people
                she cares about,

                and she *never*
                gives up on them.

EL NACI

is surrounded
by mango trees.

Brissia's almond skin
makes the freckles
on her nose stand out.

She wears denim shorts
and a pink swimsuit.

I'm already wearing my
swim shorts.

We leave our backpacks
on some rocks.
Then we walk where
the water and the stones meet.

Small green leaves fall
in the river.

None of our classmates are here.
Great!

I put my
life jacket on.

WHERE WATER IS BORN

My skin chills.
Fish nibble
my toes.

"Come on,"
Brissia whispers.
She takes my hand.

My "straws"
start kicking.
I unzip my
life jacket.
It floats in the
emerald water.

From where we are,
you can see
the entrance
to the cave where
Cihuamichin lives.

It's hard to
stay afloat
and breathe at
the same time.

I hear something coming
from the cave.
Cihuamichin singing.

Am I dreaming?

It's not the fish
that nibble
my toes. It's her
who wants to
bite my foot.

I squeeze my eyes.

I am stepping
on the stones
with my
life jacket on,
                        where water
                        is born.

"Todo está bien,"
Brissia says
softly.

DAD CALLS US

Wednesdays and Sundays.

"Dad is calling,"
Mamá sings from
the living room.

I run downstairs,
hoping this time
Dad and I won't have to
talk about sports
or school.

That's all
he talks about
since he left home.

He wants me to be someone
I'm just not.

Mamá hands me
the phone.
Papá's face
appears on
the screen.

"Hey, champ.
How have
you been?"

Before I finish
what I'm saying,
he asks,

"How's school going?
Try out for any teams?
Your mom
told me you're
trying to swim
again."

I tune myself out.

"It's fine, Dad.
School's fine."

Dad scratches
his beard.
"Um, just fine?"

I sigh and
tell him
my grades.

"You can do
better than
that, son.
When I was
your age . . ."

He wants to
be proud of me,
I know.

I want him
to be proud
of me, too,
no matter
my grades or
athletic
skills.

GOSSIP

At school,
moms stick like snails to
the school fence.
They watch
their kids
play on the field.

I hear them gossiping.

"They say he
has been
expelled from
several schools."

> "They say
> he comes from
> a dangerous town."

> "They say
> they killed
> his father for
> selling drugs."

Their gaze is
aimed at Eliam.

I can tell
Eliam knows
they are talking
about him.

*Are all those
things true?*

Eliam catches
me watching
him, too.

ACROSS THE FENCE

I'm crossing
the football field
when I see
Eliam coming
behind me.

I wish I could
say hello,
but I am lost
for words.

Someone says,
"What up?"
to him.
It's Enrique.

They bump fists.
Then Eliam keeps
walking.

Since Eliam arrived,
Enrique and
his friends have
accepted him
into their group.

Just for proving to
be as good
at soccer as them.

But
I don't think
Eliam is like
Enrique or Germán.

"Scaredy Daay-laan,"
Enrique chants.
"Do you
like Eliam?"
he blurts out.

"Wha-what?"
I stammer.

"I saw you at the
entrance. You were
staring at him."

I walk fast.
Enrique follows me.
"Course not," I say.
"I was waiting for—"

"Admit it.
Admit that you
like Eliam,"
Enrique insists.

I'm quiet.
My hands hold
my backpack tight.

"Day!" Brissia
waves at me. "Wait!"

And then, finally,
the bell rings.
Enrique quickens
his pace.

Moms don't know
what many
of us have
to deal with every day
on the other
                side of the fence.

BOTHERED

"What was that all about?"
Brissia asks me
while we put our stuff
on our desks.

I don't want to take out the
pastel markers
Mamá bought for my birthday.

I'd be embarrassed
if Enrique pointed them out
in front of Eliam and the others.

"What do you mean?"
I say, looking across the room.

Enrique talks and laughs
with Germán.
Eliam is in front of Enrique.

Brissia whispers,
"Was Enrique
bothering you?"

"No, no. We just,
um, talked."

She snorts. "Talked?
What were you talking about?"

"He just asked me what
the homework was, okay?"
I answer harshly.

Brissia studies my face.
"You sure you're okay?
Because you know
you can always go tell
Teacher Alfonso or Coach Irma."

"I am fine,"
I say with a shaky voice.

"Good morning, students!"
Teacher Alfonso shows up.

Thank goodness.

I TOSS AND TURN IN BED

Tomorrow is
the cleanup day
in El Naci.

Should I have told
Teacher Alfonso
what Enrique did today?

What if Enrique
does something
to humiliate me tomorrow?

I hug the pillow.
Then toss it away.

I say:
"Cihuamichin,
if you really own
the river, let me swim
freely in your waters, please.

I'd be embarrassed
if Eliam found out
I'm not going
further than
the shore."

My feet hit the cold limestone.
I am no longer in my room.

The Patroness of Water
looks at me from a rock.
"Come on in. Don't be afraid, kid."

"I am not a kid," I reply.

She cackles.
"Well, if you're not
a kid, prove it.
This time, you go in
by yourself. Goodbye."

She swims out into the river.

Fear is heavy,
and it is cold.
But I need to take a jump.

I do a few laps.
Fish swim around
until I see a tail,
and the fish disappear.

It's not a fish's tail,
but a snake's.

I scream.

A light flickers.
Mamá turned on
the little lamp
next to my bed.

Her hair sticks
to my sweaty
forehead.
"It was only
a bad dream."

Another nightmare.

NEAR THE RIVER

Mom grabs jute bags
from the car.

I carry my
water bottle and
hold Trueno.

We head to
the meeting point
under a *palapa*.

I'm glad
Mamá didn't ask
about my nightmare
last night.

I don't wanna
talk about it now.

I don't want her to know
my secret fears.

Parents, teachers, and students
wear shorts and T-shirts.
It's barely 9 a.m.,
and beads of sweat
break out on our faces.

Brissia and Lesly arrive together.
Lesly sighs.
"A Friday with no school.
A dream come true!"

"Do you want to go for a walk?"
Brissia asks me.

I glance down at the river.
"I'll save my energy for
today's cleanup."

She shrugs. "It's your loss.
Can I take Trueno with me?"

I think for a second.
"Just don't
take him that far.
You know how Mamá is."

As Brissia and
Lesly walk away,
I see that Eliam
has arrived.

He wears
a black T-shirt
and a white cap.
His wavy hair
spills out beneath
the cap.

He smiles.
Wait, is Eliam
smiling at me?

"Hey, Day,
what's up?"

I swallow.

ELIAM ASKS

"Why didn't you
join your friends?
Brissia and Lesly, right?"

I shrug.

I ask where
his friends are.

He shrugs.

We exchange laughs.

Across the palapa,
I find Brissia
waving at me.
She mouths
something
I can't catch.

Then she walks over
and greets Eliam.

OPERATION ANT

Coach Irma claps her hands.

"Guys, gather around.
We'll do an activity called
'Operation Ant.'"

We all listen, except Enrique,
who runs late, talking to Germán.

Coach gives instructions:

"Each team will be assigned
an area to clean.

Some of you,
the grass and forest.
Others, near the water.

Bottles, straws, and
plastic bags are sorted separately."

Brissia hushes Enrique.
"I can't hear."

"Everything alright back there?"
Coach asks.

Brissia nods.

Coach Irma has to stop
to say, "Enrique,
pay attention,
or you won't be able to play
in the river."

Parents and children make teams.

I get together with Mom,
Brissia, Brissia's mom,
and Lesly.

"Germán and his dad, you're on
Brissia's team," says Coach Irma.

Even though Germán and Lesly
are cousins, both complain.

At least I don't go with Enrique.
I turn around and realize
that neither Enrique's nor
Eliam's family came today.

TEAMING WITH GERMÁN

doesn't end up
being that bad.

He and I take care of
the disposables and
the snack bags.

      We don't talk much.

My mom and his dad collect
glass bottles
near the river.

      They even laugh.

Two hours later,
we're done
cleaning up.

Coach Irma says
we did a
good job and
gives us permission
to swim.

I grab my
backpack to
go change.

Germán walks
ahead with Enrique
and Eliam.

Only Eliam
flashes a
hearty smile.

Germán acts
like he doesn't
know me.

I guess it takes
more than a
team activity
for him to change.

THE SHARKS

We plunge
into the river.
Everyone goes
deep but me.

I stare at the rocks
at my feet.

Coach Irma
blows her whistle.
She announces
a game called
The Sharks.

Brissia helps give
the instructions:

"Everyone walks
in the shallow area,
waist-deep in water.

Coach Irma
will give everyone
a number. Next,
Lesly will call out
one of those
randomly.

The shark.

The shark must dive,
alerting everyone.

The moment
the shark catches up
with someone,
these two will
continue the hunt
together."

Lesly adds:

"Everyone
must be inside
this area.

Do not kick or
hit anyone.

Whoever isn't
caught by the sharks
wins."

Teacher Alfonso
splits us into
three groups
of eight.

He mentions
Enrique's name
in my group. I sigh.

Next, I hear
"Eliam."
I bite my nails.
I don't want
to play this,

but Coach Irma
gives me
number five.
I start to move.

"Six!" Lesly
suddenly screams.
It's Enrique. Ugh.

He doesn't
come after me.
He goes straight
for Maggy,
another classmate.

I look around.
Now Maggy
goes after Ana,

the smallest girl
in this group.

Enrique goes
after Eliam,
but can't catch
him.

I should swim
far from Enrique,
but he yells
at someone
"Get him!"

Eliam looks
at me. I freeze.

Enrique yells again,
"Get him!"

I know Enrique
won't give up.

He grabs
my legs and
turns me around.
"I got you,
Scaredy Daylan."

IN TOO DEEP

I shake my legs,
and I twist.
I don't know
why I bother.
Enrique is stronger
than me.

He takes me
by the arms
and pulls me under.

I swallow water.
I cough.

Coach Irma blows her whistle.
"Enough!"

"Day! Day!"
Some voices cheer.

Enough, I think.

But Enrique
lunges at me.
My eyes shut.

When they open,
I spy spots of
light turquoise
in the deep navy
blending together.

We're in the deep zone.

Enrique keeps
pushing me down.

"Stop! I can't breathe!"
My arms move slow.
I can't let go.

"OOOUCH!"
Suddenly,
Enrique lets out a scream
and releases me.

He looks down
and around,
not understanding
what just happened.

I do the same,
gasping for air.

Brissia and
Coach Irma
are already
swimming to us.

Brissia holds me
and yells at
Enrique, "What is
wrong with y—"

He cries out,
"Ayyy, my leg!"

He covers it with both hands.
Blood doesn't stop running.

"Easy. Maybe
you got bit by
a big fish,"
Coach Irma says.

She asks Lesly
and Eliam
to hold Enrique up.

People look down
at the water.
Eliam looks at me,
puzzled.

70

DEAR CIHUAMICHIN,

What happened today
was very strange.
I think you were there.

Although I don't know
much about fish,
I'm sure that's not
what bit Enrique.

The wound looked deep, deep.
Enrique held back the tears.
He said, "Boys don't cry."

Some classmates were joking that
I had bitten Enrique.

I don't know what Eliam thought.

Mom whispered, "Are you okay?"

I just wanted to get in the car
and cry.

I think I saw a
whirlpool form
as I sank.

Please tell me,
Cihuamichin.
Was it you who bit
Enrique?

I know
it sounds bad,
but if it was you,
gracias.
I thought he
would drown me.

If it was you,
gracias.
Because today
I found out
I can dive.

If it was you,
gracias,
because on Sunday
when Papá calls,
I'll tell him
I swam.

ACCIDENTS

"Wake up.
Someone's calling you,"
Mamá says.
She shakes my shoulder
softly.

I barely
open my eyes.
It's Papá.

He tells me
he's proud of me
because I'm
swimming again.
That makes me
feel good.

Papá talks about
how the company
he works for
fired an "idiot" for nearly
blowing up a car.

"Is the man
alright?" I ask.

Papá nods,
"Yeah, yeah.
It was just a scare."

Then I realize

> Dad didn't ask if
> Enrique was okay.
>
> Dad didn't ask if
> *I* was okay.

Now there are
two people hurt.

> Enrique,
> for the "fish bite."
>
> Me, because Papá
> didn't think
> about how I felt.
> This was an accident,
> after all.

I ESCAPE

to our yard
to play with Trueno.

I don't want
to talk about
Dad's call with Mamá.

"Time for breakfast!"
Mom yells.
She also says
excitedly,

"Brissia texted
to invite you to picnic
by the river!"

After what happened
on Friday, I don't
feel like going.

Mom insists
it's a good idea.

I prepare
my backpack–
swim shorts,
water shoes, and a towel.

Outside,
a car horn blows.

"*Ándale*. They're here."

Mom waves and
smiles at
Brissia's parents.
They're in
the front seats.

I say hi and
jump in the back
of the truck.

HEAT WAVE

We scramble out
of the pickup truck.
The sun beats down.

"Uff, what a heat wave!"
Brissia's mom opens
a paper fan.
"I'll just sit around
for the rest
of the day."

"Mmm, looks like
you're from Antarctica,"
Mr. Olvera jokes.

Brissia, Lesly,
and I laugh.

"And the heat wave
just began."
Brissia's mom says.

SWIMMERS

I forgot my life jacket,
so I sit on the shore.

Brissia moves her legs.
"Come on, Day, you already did it!
And you can't just
forget how to swim."

Lesly nods. "Besides, Brissia
and I are great swimmers.
If something happened . . ."

Brissia shakes her head.
"Nothing will happen.
He's a swimmer, too."

She's right. I am a swimmer.
I've been swimming
since I was a baby.

It's just that the weight
of my fears of Cihuamichin
weigh me down.

The secrets in these waters
threaten to drown me.

At first, I tread water.
Then, I let my body
fall in.
My arms circle.

Brissia grins.

The water sparkles
with the glimmer
of sunlight.

> I exhale and glide
> over to Brissia.
> "Thank you,"
> I mumble.

> She and Lesly hug me.
> I'm already
> crying.

AS WE SWIM

I tell Brissia and Lesly that
I think Cihuamichin
was the one who attacked
Enrique.

I'm embarrassed to admit it.

"No way!" Lesly blurts out.
"How can you believe
Cihuamichin really exists?"

Brissia says,
"Well, it could have been anything.
Even a rock."

"That wasn't a rock.
It was a bite," I state.

Lesly continues,
"Even if she was real,
why would she come to defend *you*?"

"I don't think she came to defend *me*,"
I explain.

"Maybe she just doesn't like it
when people cause trouble
in her waters."

"Still sounds kind of . . ."
Brissia pauses.
I'm waiting for her to say
"childish."
But instead, she says "loony."

"Do you think the others
still think that
I attacked Enrique?"

I want to ask,
Do you think Eliam thinks
I'd attack his friend?

Lesly shakes her head.
"Nah. You couldn't.
I mean, I saw the wound,
and it was awful."

"I think Eliam
was the most
surprised," I say.

Lesly moves closer to me.
"Day, can I ask you
something?"

My heart thuds.
I think I know
what she'll ask,
but I nod.

"Do you have
a crush on—?"

Brissia splashes at Lesly.
"Hey, look!"

My eyes travel
to the other side
of the river.

A couple of
pickup trucks are
unloading coolers,
plastic bags, and
fishing rods.

Right where it says

NO FISHING
IN THIS AREA.

And crossing the river,
I spot Enrique, Germán,
their dads—

and Eliam.

ABUELO'S STORY

Abuelo told me stories
about when he was young—
back when people
in San José Lagos
used to fish all week.

One day, they realized
fish began to dwindle.
There were days when all they
caught was dehydration and heat.

The townspeople spread
the rumor that they had angered
the Patroness of Water.
They placed signs around the rivers:
NO FISHING IN THIS AREA

It took over 20 years for
Cihuamichin to bring
fish back.

But at least Abuelo could see
life under the water
reborn before he was gone.

CROSSING

"Should we try crossing?"
Lesly asks.

Brissia's gaze
drifts from where
the trucks are
        toward Enrique's dad,
        who is grilling
        meat.

"Um, that
would be risky,"
Brissia says.

I bite my nails.
"I don't think
I can make it.
I'm just getting back
to swimming."

"Food is ready!"
Brissia's mom
announces from her
picnic spot.
She places carne asada
in a bowl.

I grab my towel.
I set quesadillas
and guacamole
on a plate.

Brissia's parents
eat under a palapa.

Brissia, Lesly, and I
settle by the river
with our food.

I watch a family
ride on a *lancha*,
laughing.
An empty lancha
sits next to them.

As if reading
my thoughts,
Lesly says,

"We should
get in that boat."

LA CHALUPA

Mr. Olvera watches
the wooden boat—
white peeling paint—
with concern.
"No way."

"Dad, please.
We just want to
cross and come back,"
Brissia whines.

Mr. Olvera frowns
at her. "Who do you
think you are,
La Chalupa?"

Lesly and I can't
help but laugh.

Brissia's mom says,
"No. Besides,
you don't know
who's on the
other side."

"It's just our
classmates," Brissia says.

"Actually,
my uncle and
cousin Germán
are there,"
Lesly adds.

"Why do you you want
to go there, huh?"
Mr. Olvera asks.

I sigh.
"Because they are fishing.
Someone needs
to tell them
that's forbidden."

I'm surprised
at myself for
speaking up.

They let us go.

WHILE ROWING

I avoid Lesly's gaze.

But when I look up at her,
she immediately
says, "I know
you like Eliam."

My stomach clenches.
"No?! I—I don't . . ."

Brissia is in the front.
She keeps
rowing calmly.
"Leave him
alone, Lesly."

Brissia knows
I like Eliam.

Lesly says,
"Ay, well, sorry!
I just saw how
you looked at Eliam
the other day."

I let out a breath.

"I'm not sure
how I feel.
Maybe I just wish
we were friends."

My paddle
hits a glass bottle.
Brissia's hits
the ground.

The boat rocks.

Eliam, Germán,
and Enrique
are on the shore.

UNPROTECTED LAND

"What are you doing here?"
Enrique snorts.

Brissia crouches down
and picks up an
empty snack bag.

"Excuse me? What
are you doing here
with those?"
She points to the fishing rods
stacked on a pickup truck.

"Having a good time with
the family,"
Germán says, laughing.

Lesly approaches him.
"Do you know you guys can
get in trouble
for being here?"

Enrique turns to me.
"Ah. Let me guess.
You came to see someone."

Eliam shoots me a look.
My heart pounds.

"Enrique, stop,"
Brissia says sharply.

I'm glad that Germán's dad
comes over and greets Lesly,
surprised to see her here.

A cloud of smoke
billows into the blue sky.
"You guys are just in time
for the fried mojarra fish."

As we walk,
my feet come across
Coke cans, plastic bags,
and glass bottles.

This is the land
we should protect.

All of a sudden,
I feel my heart
being squeezed.

STOLEN

Enrique's dad
puts cooking oil in a
plow disc.

Eliam opens
the cooler to take
the mojarras out.
He startles.

I take a look.
There are dozens
of fish inside.
Some of them
glimmer in different
shades as if
they were made
of living metal.

Is it the sunlight . . .
or are they moving?

"Actually, we
need to get back,"
Lesly tells
her uncle.

"Those fish look . . .
weird," Brissia
whispers to me.

Because they are
                not for eating.
Because they do not
                belong to us.
Because they were
                stolen from the river.

Before I say a word,
I hear sirens.

THE WRONG PEOPLE

When Papá talks
on the phone
with Mamá,
he always tells her:

she should
take care of herself
and take care of me.

And she shouldn't
mess with the
wrong people.

I wonder
what would happen
if Mom and Dad
found out that
Brissia's parents
let us paddle here.

And that we are
messing with the
state police.

Before the
state police arrive,
Enrique and
Germán quickly put
the fishing rods away.

Eliam hesitantly
closes the cooler
and drags it along
the river stones.

Germán's dad calls
Brissia's parents
to let them know
we are fine.

The oil pops
on the disc.
It's too late
to put the fire out.

Two police
officers get close.

Brissia, Lesly,
and I stand still.

"You know that
fishing is prohibited
in this area, right?"
a police officer
asks Germán's dad.

Before he speaks,
another police
officer talks to Eliam.
"A ver, mijo.
Bring that cooler to me."

Enrique's father curses.
"You guys
don't even do
anything for this town,
so don't come
around and scr—"

When I hear
Enrique's dad,
I understand
why his son
is the way he is.

THE CONFUSION

on their faces
makes me look
into the cooler.
No fish inside.

The police search
the grass to see
if Eliam has
dumped them
there, but there's no trace.

I look out to the river.

Colorful spots flicker in the water.
"Look!" I shout
at my friends.

But when they get closer,
everything seems
normal again.

Brissia's parents' truck pulls up.
Brissia and I are
headed home.

THAT NIGHT

It feels like I'm falling
into deep water.
The bottom is dark.

The soles of
my feet tickle.

When I open my eyes,
sunlight shows lines
of fish moving
under me.

"They're saying
goodbye, Day,"
says a voice
that gets closer
and closer.

I know it's
Cihuamichin even when
all I see are
blurred lines.

"Saying goodbye?
Where are they going?"
I ask her, shocked.

"They are tired.
You humans
have not respected
my rules.

You throw garbage.
You fish in
protected areas.
All of this will have
consequences."

I don't know why
my mind replays
the day
my dad left,
me crying as
I see him go.

Someone shakes me.

"My child,
you are only
dreaming."

I open my eyes.
I'm in Mom's arms,
sobbing.

NOT A FISH

Papá calls me
on the way to
the supermarket.

Mom tells me
not to tell him
about what happened yesterday,
so I don't.

We head to the entrance.
I see a guy
helping a woman
carry some bags.

It's Eliam and his mom.
He waves.

"Is he the boy
in your class?
The one that . . ."
Mom mumbles.

I cut her off.
"Yeah. Eliam."

Mamá greets his mother,
who wears a long skirt
and her hair in a
thick braid.

I try not to stare
at Eliam.
"Are you okay?
I mean . . ."
My voice cracks.

Eliam knows what
I'm talking
about. He nods.

"It's just
something weird
happened. While
we were fishing,
Enrique's dad
tried to catch something . . .
but it didn't
look like a fish.
The tail was huge.
It made the whole
boat shake.
I got scared."

"Day, are you
ready?" Mom smiles
at Eliam.

I stare,
blank-faced.

I just hear
Eliam's mom
saying, "Adiós!"

CONSEQUENCES

On Monday, after
flag ceremony,
Teacher Alfonso
enters the classroom
with a serious look.

He takes
his glasses off
and sighs,
"Guys, I have bad news.
The annual swimming
competition
has been canceled."

Everyone groans.

"The second piece of bad news . . .
is the reason why.

Germán's dad was hospitalized
on Saturday.
He got heatstroke
while he was coming home
from the river.

This heat wave is just too intense.
We can't risk more people
being hurt. Or worse."

Slight murmurs
float through the
classroom.

Brissia looks at me and
mouths, "What?"

"Is he okay?"
someone asks.

"Well, fortunately,
Germán and Lesly
were with him
in the truck.
They got help
just in time."

After the incident
with the police
on Saturday,
Germán's dad
said he'd take
Lesly back home.

I had gone with Brissia
and her parents.

"Guys, stay
hydrated and try not
to spend too much
time in the sun,"
Teacher Alfonso says.
"It hasn't rained in months.
The heat wave is worse
than it has been
in years."

The first thing
I think of is
Cihuamichin's legend:

*Breaking
her rules has
consequences.*

AT RECESS

Brissia and I
stay in
the classroom.

"I need to tell
you something,"
I say.

"What is it?"
she asks, worried.

"It's about
Cihuamichin."

Brissia sighs.

"I know you didn't believe me
when I told you.
When we were nine," I say.
"Now you probably
think it's a child's
thing, but listen.
Yesterday, I ran into Eliam."

Brissia's smile widens. "Uh-huh?"

I click my teeth.
"No. Listen, please."

Then I tell her
what Eliam told me, and
about the fish in the cooler.
"Don't you think it's strange that
they suddenly disappeared?"

"Daylan, it took a while
for the state police to arrive.
Eliam had enough time to . . ."

The classroom door squeaks.
We both turn.
Eliam and Enrique are standing there.

THEY HEARD
WHAT I'D SAID

"You really think she exists?"
Enrique mocks.
I stare at the floor.

Enrique continues.
"I mean, I knew
you were a scaredy cat
and that you were g—"

"I believe in her, too,"
Eliam cuts him off.

My stomach clenches.

"What?"
Enrique snorts.

"I believe in her, too,"
Eliam repeats.
"First, the lancha moving.
Then, the cooler.
When I opened it,
the fish were
no longer there."

Brissia asks,
"So why didn't you
say anything?"

Eliam sighs.
"I was scared.
And then the incident
with Germán's dad …"

"*Neta*, do you believe
in all that or
are you just trying to
make Daylan
feel better?"

Eliam rolls his eyes.
"What do you mean?"

"Because Daylan likes you,"
Enrique snaps.

Brissia and I
stare at Eliam, stunned.
His expression is
neither surprised
nor angry.

I feel dizzy.

The bell rings.
Recess is over.

I want to puke.

Eliam pushes Enrique.
"From now on,
we're no longer
friends, okay?"

Enrique laughs
awkwardly. "Why?"

"Why do you enjoy
making people
feel bad?" Eliam asks.

Before Enrique
responds, Eliam
walks away.

AT DISMISSAL

I race to the
school entrance.
Brissia is behind me.
"Hey. Are you
alright?"

I nod, but tears
quickly flood
my eyes.

"Ay, Day."
She takes napkins
out of her backpack
and wipes my tears.
"It's okay."

"I hate being
called out like that,"
I say, sniffling.

Brissia nods,
and then she
hugs me tight.

LESLY LIVES

a few blocks from school.
An almond tree
covers her patio.
Her two dogs,
Juancho and Cuca,
are playing under
its branches.
Three chickens cluck.

Lesly sits on a plastic chair.
Brissia and I sit next to her.

Brissia fills her in
on everything we know.

Lesly nods.
"It was weird, guys,
what happened
to my uncle.
We were in his truck,
and he started
sweating a lot.
He turned red
and said he felt
like he couldn't breathe.

Then he turned
the truck off.
His head hit
the steering wheel."

"Is he better now?"
Brissia asks.
Lesly nods.

Brissia asks me,
"What do you think
she wants? Cihuamichin."

"Maybe she just
wants us to leave
her waters alone,"
I say.

"Something doesn't make sense,"
Lesly says.
"If she wanted revenge,
why did this only
happen to my uncle?
Enrique's father was
the one who came up
with the idea of fishing."

I don't know the answer
to that.

The chickens
cluck louder.

Lesly says,
"My *abuela* says that
chickens announce
the arrival of a storm
with an unusual
cackling.
And this sounds weird.
Maybe we should
go inside."

THE SKY TURNS HAZY

It drums loudly
as if it's going to fall.
Mom and I drop Brissia
at her house.

When we open
the door, Trueno
is crying, scared.
Mamá lets him
stay inside.
I give him a hug.

"I'll make us food.
Ay, I hope the power
doesn't go out."

Mom's phone rings.
"Answer, Day.
It must be your dad."

"It's Brissia,"
I say as I walk
up the stairs.

"Something happened."
Brissia sounds upset.

"Is everything
alright?" I ask.

"I just spoke
to Germán," she says.
"I asked him
how his dad
was doing.
And he told me
that Enrique
had invited him
to El Naci today."

"Today?
In this storm?" I ask.

"Daylan, my phone!"
Mom yells from downstairs.

"Well, the point is,
Germán called Enrique,
but he sent it to voicemail.

What if Cihuamichin
has decided that,
instead of taking
revenge on
Enrique's dad . . ."

Suddenly,
everything clicks.
The bite that
Enrique got
in the river.
My dreams.
The legend.

" . . . she would
take revenge
on his son,"
I think aloud.

"And wait,"
Brissia says.
"Apparently Enrique
didn't go alone.
Eliam is with him."

RAINDROPS BEAT HARD

against my window.

"We have to
make sure
they're okay, Bris."

"Have you seen
how it is outside?" she asks.

"I know it's
the worst idea ever,
but we're not
that far from
El Naci by bike."

Brissia huffs.
"Twenty minutes
in this weather is far."

"Then I'll go by myself,"
I say.

Brissia sighs loudly.

LYING

Mom says,
"I'll heat up the food."
She likes to make
caldo de res
when it rains.

We haven't had it
in a long time.

After a few
spoonfuls, I say,
"I'm full."

"Are you okay?
You hardly ate."

"I'm just tired.
I think
I'll take a nap."

Mom watches
me carefully,
as if she knows
I'm hiding something
from her.

"You almost
never nap."

"I'm tired, Mom."
I pretend to yawn.

"Alright then.
I'll finish
cleaning down here."

My heart
beats hard.
I can barely breathe.

I don't like
lying to Mamá.
As soon as I hear
her playing music
on her phone,
I tiptoe downstairs.

I WRITE A NOTE

Mom,

I had to go.
I have to help
two friends.
I've gone to El Naci.
I'm not going alone.
Brissia will be
with me.
It won't take us long.

Love you,
Day

P.S. I'm sorry.

"Sorry,
little buddy,"
I say to Trueno.
"I can't risk anything
happening to you."

Trueno stands
crying at the
back door while
I run away.

THE SKY IS DARK

It doesn't look
like it's four
in the afternoon.

I meet Brissia
at the corner
of her block.

There is no one
on the street.

Only the cars
that pass by,
splashing us.

The rain is
easing up a bit.

Brissia looks up
at the sky.
"You know we'll
both be grounded
for a long time, right?"

I let out a sigh.

DROPLETS HIT MY FACE

Brissia pedals
faster than me.
"Come on, Day.
Keep up."

We are totally
soaked. I'm not sure
if we'll get there.

I'm not sure if this
was a good idea.

I get scared
when I see
big pickup trucks.

We could run
into bad people.

We keep moving forward.

A DANGEROUS ROAD

The dirt road to El Naci
is full of large puddles.

A white Chevy
Silverado rushes by
and sprays us with muddy water.

I concentrate on pedaling.

I focus on getting there.

To Eliam.

We are almost
there when,
in the distance,
we hear screams.

They're nearly drowned out
by the sound of the wind.

We leave the bikes
and start running,
stumbling,
falling.

THE CAVE

We run near
the entrance
to the river's cave.

In the deepest area,
Eliam tries
to hold Enrique.

The current is too strong.

Brissia takes her shoes off
and dives into
the water.

I just keep
watching.
I don't know
what to do.

The words
Daylan Little Straws
Scaredy Daylan
Daylan can't swim
come to my mind.

If I don't
jump in, Brissia
won't be able
to hold both
of them.

Brissia tries
to grab Enrique,
but the water
pulls him under.

Eliam tries
to stay afloat,
but the rain
comes down again.

Oh no!

I can see only Eliam's
hands above the water.

I jump.

MY FEARS ARE
WASHED AWAY

as I hold onto Eliam.

"I've got you,"
I whisper.
Water comes out
of his nose.
He coughs.

His hands are cut,
as if he had tried
to hold on to something.

His chest moves—
he's breathing.
I try to hold
onto a tree.
The current's stronger
than me.

"Eliam, wake up."
I shake his shoulders
roughly.

"Please, Cihuamichin,
help me," I beg.

FOREVER

I look toward
Brissia, who has
her back turned.

She climbs onto
a stone ledge
with Enrique
in her arms,
his eyes half-closed.

"Cihuamichin,
Eliam is not to
blame for anything."
My tears roll
down Eliam's
pale face.

A song comes
from the cave.

Brissia turns, open-mouthed.

The Patroness of Water
rises above
the river.

She doesn't have
a fish tail, nor legs.
Instead, a white gown
floats through
the water.

A crown of
shining stones rests
on her head.
Her long hair
covers almost
her entire body.

Her honey skin is
delicate, like a paper
about to tear.

Her gaze lands
on Eliam.
Her hands open.

Then I remember
the legend:
*For those offenders,
she would
entangle them
and drag them
to the depths
forever.*

"She's coming
for Eliam.
She'll take him
with her, Brissia!"

I can't stop
crying.

My body loosens.
I can't hold Eliam
any longer.

I think of
Papá and Mamá.
Eliam's mom
that I only met
yesterday.

I release him.

The Patroness of Water
holds both
me and Eliam.
Her arms feel cold.

"NOOOO!"
Brissia screams.

I feel the water
entering my lungs
as I sink into
the depths of El Naci.

The waters close.

MY LUNGS EMPTY

Dead fish
float in the
cloudy water.

"What happened
to them?" I ask.
My voice echoes.

"Breathe,"
a voice says.

I plunge
into the abyss.

With a
white face
and purple hands,
Eliam is lying
in the water.

I shout.

BREATHE

White light.
Like a hospital.
But it smells
like home.

My cheeks
feel wet.

"It's okay, baby.
Just breathe."
The same voice.

It's Mamá.

Am I dreaming?
Was this all just another dream?

No. No. This happened.

Another voice says,
"I love you."

It's Papá.

Am I dreaming?

When I open
my eyes, I'm in
Mom's bed.
Trueno is moving
his head, confused.

"Where is Eliam?" I sob.

Dad and Mom grin.

"What?" I ask, scared.

Dad says,
"Calm down. He's fine."

Mom's fingers
play with my hair.
"He spent the night
in the hospital.
He swallowed
a lot of water,
but he'll be fine."

"Can I go see him?"
I try to get up.

Mom hugs me.
"Yes, we can,
but you have
to rest first, okay?"

"And Brissia? And Enrique?"

"Ah, they're fine, too.
 I'm glad you're okay, my boy,"
Mom says, sobbing.

Dad gently squeezes
my shoulder.

"Day, there's something I have
to tell you."

"Day, it doesn't matter
who you are,
nor what you are
good at.
For me, you are
the best.
You will always
be loved by us."

I swallow hard.

It's all I wanted
to hear.

I choke out,
"I'll always
love you, too."

Papá and Mamá
hug me tight.

That's all it takes
for my eyes to start
watering again.

Finally,
my body relaxes.

A WEEK LATER

the Cihuamichin
celebrations resume.

Little by little,
the fish return.
San José Lagos
is filled with life.

We paint
the night with
colorful paper flags
with shapes of
the fish lady
and candles.

It smells like
tamales, pozole,
flowers, and *copal*.

Dancers perform
the ancestral dances
for Cihuamichin.

At the end of
the dance,
the president of
San José Lagos
asks the people
to gather in
the main palapa.

He cheerfully says
through the
microphone,

"Given the
circumstances,
this year we did not
hold the swimming
competition.

However, two great
young people
showed that,
in addition
to having a good heart,
they are brave.

Brissia Olvera
and Daylan Torres,
I ask you to
come forward."

People shout
and applaud.
My hands are sweating.
My heart pounds.

Seeing everyone
who supports me—
my parents,
        Eliam, Lesly,
Teacher Alfonso—
I have a feeling
that no matter what happens,

I will be okay.

Coach Irma
and the president's wife place
some fake tiaras on us.
They look like
the ones in the drawings
of Cihuamichin.

If only they knew.

DAZZLING LASERS

light up
the starry sky.
They announce
the end of the
celebration.

Some families
start to leave.
Others stay and
keep chatting.

I tell my parents
I'll look
for Brissia.
I take Trueno
with me.

I sit under a tree.
"Hey." It's Eliam's voice.

"Can I join you?"
he asks with
a wide smile.

I laugh and nod.

After the incident at the river,
we haven't had time to talk.
The day I went to his house,
our parents never
left us alone.

It makes sense.

That day I found out
that he lives
only with his mom.

That his father
didn't die like
the townspeople say.

His dad died in an accident
while he was driving home.
He was a truck driver.

I let his mom tell their story.

Besides, it wouldn't
make sense to talk
about what
happened to us.

They would
call us crazy.

We sit quietly
while Eliam pets Trueno.
Then he says,

"I wanted to tell
you something."
He looks me
right in the eye.

"Daylan, you're . . .
after all this
that happened,
you're like my best friend.
You know that,
right?"

Adrenaline pumps
through my body.
"Um, yeah?"

"Well, yeah, I mean . . .
I like . . . "

"Hey! Hey!"
Brissia yells.

I sigh. Eliam runs
a hand through
his messy hair.

I look down.
Brissia points to a rock
that stands out
in the river. "Look
over there!"

I follow
the direction
where Brissia
is pointing.

Trueno barks.

Then I see it—
a fish tail,
the same one
I saw three years ago,
sticking out.

As soon as it's there, it's gone.
Leaving only black waves
behind it.

AUTHOR'S NOTE

Mexico is a multicultural and multiethnic country. As in most cultures, for the Mexican indigenous peoples, water is a fundamental part of the sacred, mythological, artistic, and technological spheres. The way they perceive the world is defined by a deep commitment to environmental conservation. Depending on the region, stories have emerged from oral tradition related to the element of water.

In collaboration with Professor Enrique Sánchez, I decided to create the fictional character of Cihuamichin, respecting and valuing the stories of oral tradition and the characters that have been already created by indigenous groups in Mexico.

Cihuamichin is a word of Nahuatl origin that is derived from two words: 'cihuatl' (women) and 'michin' (fish).

Want to Keep Reading?

Here's a sneak peek at another book
from West 44 Books:

Liam and the Giant Eels
by Ann Malaspina

ISBN#: 9781978597549

THE GREEN CHAIR

The green chair
       on the deck
             stood empty.

       No one touched it.
       No one sat in it.

They pretended it wasn't there.

Just like the stuff
       in Gramps's bedroom.

One evening in July,
       a bird
            landed
                 in the chair.

"Could it be an osprey?" Liam asked.

Gramps loved watching the ospreys
       fly along Blackwater Creek.

"It's only a gull," Mom said.

One of a million scavengers
       begging for scraps
       at the Jersey Shore.

Bummer.

EARLY MORNING

at Sandy Cove Beach,

      Pink bubblegum sky.

      Joggers (including Mom)
           on the boardwalk.

      Matt the lifeguard, half-asleep.

      Umbrellas opened
           on the white sand.

And a flat, green, boring ocean.

WAITING

Liam floated
on his boogie board.

Waiting for
something—
anything—
to happen.

What a loser of a summer.

No waves.
No friends.
No blue crabs in his crab pot.
No Gramps.

A Jet Ski shot past Liam.

His board flipped
like a pancake.

"Way to go, Liam!"

Matt the lifeguard
put up his thumb.

ROSIE

"Hey, folks! Got any paintings for me?"

> A woman in a huge blue dress
> was setting up the Art Tent
> on the boardwalk.

Gramps's old friend, Rosie.

> Coco, the parrot,
> sat on her shoulder.
> He was eating a grape.

Mom shook her head. "Sorry, Rosie, not today."

> Liam had noticed Mom
> wasn't painting much this summer.

Rosie peered at him.

"Seen anything odd, young Liam?"

TIMES LIKE THIS

Rosie leaned on her cane.
"What about the crabs?"

How did Rosie know about the crabs?

Liam's crab pot
had been empty for weeks.

"Something odd is going on."
Rosie shook her head.

"Times like this,
I wish your gramps were here."

And now she was reading Liam's mind!

Lifting his wings, Coco squawked.
"Keep your eyes peeled!"

Nora Wright and the Secrets of The Knight

MAX HOWARD

KATY GRANT

DISASTER TRAIL

DJ BRANDON

TELL ME WHY THE JACK PINE GROWS

MY OWN SPIN

DAVID ARO

CHECK OUT MORE BOOKS AT:
www.west44books.com

ABOUT THE AUTHOR

Edd Tello is the author of the young adult books *Only Pieces* (2022) and *No Place for Fairy Tales* (2023) from West 44 Books. Both titles are Junior Library Guild Gold Standard Selections. Edd holds a master's degree in creative writing from the University of Seville. When he isn't reading or writing, you'll find him drinking coffee or making his friends laugh with his unfortunate anecdotes and jokes. Edd currently lives in Vancouver, Canada. You can find him online at eddtello.com, and @eddstello on socials.